Ann

Raggedy Ann and Andy

and the

Magic Potion

ADAPTED BY STEPHANIE TRUE PETERS
FROM THE STORIES BY JOHNNY GRUELLE

ILLUSTRATED BY REG SANDLAND

SIMON & SCHUSTER BOOKS FOR YOUNG READERS
NEW YORK   LONDON   TORONTO   SYDNEY   SINGAPORE

SIMON & SCHUSTER BOOKS FOR YOUNG READERS

 An imprint of Simon & Schuster Children's Publishing Division

1230 Avenue of the Americas, New York, New York 10020

The text of this book is set in Jenson.

The illustrations are rendered in watercolor and ink.

Printed in the United States of America

10 9 8 7 6 5 4 3 2 1

Library of Congress Cataloging-in-Publication Data

My first Raggedy Ann : Raggedy Ann and Andy and the magic potion : adapted from stories by Johnny Gruelle / illustrated by Reg Sandland.

p.   cm.

"Based on stories previously published in Raggedy Ann and the happy meadow . . ."—T.p. verso.

Summary: After taking a special potion, Raggedy Ann and Raggedy Andy are able to see and talk to all the magic meadow folk around them.

ISBN 0-689-83180-3

[1. Dolls Fiction. 2. Magic Fiction. 3. Fairies Fiction.]

I. Gruelle, Johnny, 1880?-1938. Raggedy Ann and the happy meadow.

II. Sandland, Reg, ill.

PZ7.M97625 2001   [E]—dc21   99-31289

The History of Raggedy Ann

One day, a little girl named Marcella discovered an old rag doll in her attic.
Because Marcella was often ill and had to spend much of her time at home,
her father, a writer named Johnny Gruelle, looked for ways to keep her entertained.
He was inspired by Marcella's rag doll, which had bright shoe-button eyes and
red yarn hair. The doll became known as Raggedy Ann.

Knowing how much Marcella adored Raggedy Ann, Johnny Gruelle wrote
stories about the doll. He later collected the stories he had written for Marcella and
published them in a series of books. He gave Raggedy Ann a brother, Raggedy Andy,
and over the years the two rag dolls acquired many friends.

Raggedy Ann has been an important part of Americana for more than half a century,
as well as a treasured friend to many generations of readers. After all, she is much more
than a rag doll—she is a symbol of caring and love, of compassion and generosity.
Her magical world is one that promises to delight
children of all ages for years to come.

One fine spring day, Raggedy Ann and Raggedy Andy walked to the Looking Glass Brook in Happy Meadow. Suddenly, a puff of wind snatched Raggedy Andy's hat from his head. Raggedy Ann and Raggedy Andy chased it, but every time they came close to catching it, another gust blew it beyond their reach.

The Raggedys soon grew too tired to chase it anymore. They sat down and watched the wind toss the hat this way, then that way.

"I think your hat is the only thing the wind is playing with!" Raggedy Ann said. And it was true! The grass beneath the hat didn't move, and neither did the leaves on the trees above it.

"Then how can we ever catch it?" moaned Raggedy Andy.

Just then, the Raggedys heard a low, rumbling laugh. It was Grandpa Hoppytoad.

Grandpa Hoppytoad held up a small glass bottle. "I have something here I think will help you," he croaked. "It's a special potion. With one drop, you'll be able to see all the magic folk of the meadow. Then you'll see what's happening to Raggedy Andy's hat."

Raggedy Ann laughed. "That's wonderful! But with our mouths painted on, how can we take the potion?"

Grandpa Hoppergrass leaped from the grass behind them. "I have an idea."

He told Raggedy Ann to lean her head down to him. With a quick flick of his back leg, which was like a tiny saw, he cut a little hole in her mouth. Then he did the same for Raggedy Andy. Neither of the Raggedys felt a thing because their heads were stuffed with soft cotton.

Grandpa Hoppytoad squirted magic potion into the holes. Aunt Sophia Spider, who was spinning a web nearby, sewed up the holes neat and tidy.

The magic worked right away.

"O-o-o-h!" cried Raggedy Ann and Raggedy Andy together, for now they could see all the magic meadow folk, plain as day. Here on the water a pair paddled a leaf boat. There beneath the mushroom slept a tiny old fellow with a long white beard. And there, pulling Raggedy Andy's hat this way and that, flew the prettiest winged damsels they had ever seen!

Raggedy Ann and Raggedy Andy laughed at the trick the flying magic meadow folk had played on them.

As the magic meadow folk flew the hat back to Raggedy Andy, Raggedy Ann spied a little man dressed in brown from his acorn cap to his oak leaf shoes. Every so often, he jumped up and kissed an orange-red tiger lily. Each time he did, he left behind a teeny brown spot.

Raggedy Ann clapped her hands. "So you're the one who decorates the lilies!"

The little man winked. "You guessed it. My kiss gives the ladybug her spots, too, and the speckled trout his speckles, and baby birds their patchwork feathers."

Raggedy Andy's eyes twinkled. "I bet I can guess another kind of spot his kiss leaves behind. Freckles!"

Raggedy Ann laughed. "Surely all the little boys and girls who hate their freckles will like them better once they know a magic kiss made them!" she cried.

Raggedy Ann and Raggedy Andy walked farther into the meadow to see what other magic folk they could meet. Hand in hand, they followed the path through the waving grass and delicate wildflowers. Suddenly, they heard a frantic buzzing sound.

"It's Helen Honeybee, collecting nectar for her basket," Raggedy Ann said, spying their busy friend.

"She sounds upset," Raggedy Andy said. "Come on!"

"Oh dear, oh dear," hummed Helen Honeybee. "I think I hear a voice calling for help, but I can't see anyone. Do you hear or see anything?"

The two Raggedys listened very carefully. Thanks to the magic potion, they could hear the voice too.

"Help! Help me!" it cried.

They searched high and low. Suddenly, Raggedy Ann picked up an acorn. "The voice is coming from in here!" she cried.

Raggedy Andy held the acorn to his ear and listened to the small voice. "Look," he said, pointing to a small hole filled with pine needles and mud. "Whoever is in there is trapped!"

"Oh, what will we do?" Raggedy Ann said, looking at her mittenlike hands sadly. "We don't have fingers to pull the pine needles free."

"Let me help," Helen Honeybee said. Quickly, she used her six strong legs to dig the hole clear. Out popped the tiniest little boy they had ever seen. He was dressed head to toe in soft, white daisy petals.

"Thank you," the wee child said. "I have been shut up in that acorn all morning. I am so hungry and thirsty." Helen Honeybee gave him her basket of nectar to drink. The boy gulped it all down in one swallow and handed the empty basket back to Helen. Helen gave a small sigh, for though she was happy to have helped the boy, it had taken her two days to collect that nectar.

"Who put you in that acorn?" Raggedy Andy asked.

"I did!" a voice behind them said angrily. "Who told you you could let him out?"

The Raggedys, Helen, and the daisy child spun around. It was Snoopy Doodjinipper the Witch! The little meadow boy clung to Helen Honeybee.

"Don't let her put me in the acorn again!" he cried.

Now Mrs. Snoopy wasn't very big, but she was mad. She swatted at Helen Honeybee with all her might. Then she gave a yelp.

"Ow-oo-ow!" the witch cried. She flapped her hand in the air and danced around in a circle.

Helen Honeybee pulled out her sewing kit and peeked inside. "Just as I thought," she said. "My sharpest sewing needle is stuck in Mrs. Snoopy's finger."

Mrs. Snoopy sat with a *thump* on the ground. "Can't you pull the needle out?" she asked the Raggedys hopefully.

"Tell us why you shut the little meadow boy in the acorn first," Raggedy Ann said.

"He was swimming in my clam shell of rainwater," the witch replied, "and he didn't ask me if he could play in it."

Raggedy Ann laughed. "Is that all?"

She turned to the teeny boy. "Do you promise never to swim in Mrs. Snoopy's clam shell again unless she says you may?"

The little child nodded.

"And do you promise never to lock up another one of the magic meadow folk in an acorn again?" Raggedy Ann asked the witch.

"I promise," said the witch. "But what about my finger?"

Raggedy Ann carefully put the tiny boy on the ground. Helen Honeybee buzzed forward to Mrs. Snoopy's finger. She took hold of the sewing needle in her strong legs and pulled it free.

"Oh, thank you!" Mrs. Snoopy said. "How can I repay you?"

Helen Honeybee picked up her empty nectar basket. "You can help me fill this up again!"

The Raggedys laughed. Out of nowhere, magic meadow folk appeared—shimmering damsels darting to and fro, tiny old men and women wearing mushroom hats to keep off the sun, and a parade of leaf boats on which floated fifty baskets.

"We'll all help you!" the meadow folk cried happily. So the Raggedys and their new friends spent the rest of the day frolicking in the meadow and filling basket after basket with nectar.